I have this little sister Lola.
She is small and very funny.
Sometimes when we go to the shops Mum says
we can choose one thing as a treat.
Lola always says... chocolate.

Lola says,
"I really, extremely do like chocolate.
I like
chocolate
buttons,
chocolate eggs
and
chocolate money.

I like cake that is chocolate,
with chocolate in the middle
and on the outsidey bits too.

I like chocolate in the
shape of animals

and chocolate in the
shape of
shapes."

I say,
"But I bet you don't know where
chocolate comes from."

Lola says,
"Oh yes I do know where
chocolate comes from.
The shops."

I say, "Uh-uh, chocolate comes
actually from a tree."

Charlie

Lola says,
"I didn't know that there was an **actual**,
in fact, chocolate tree which
grows chocolate.

I might grow one in our garden
and maybe
chocolate
flowers
too...

and perhaps I will get a chocolate house."

And I say,
    "No, there isn't a tree made out of chocolate. It's just
a tree that grows giantish pods and it's called a cocoa tree.

Inside the pods
are cocoa beans and the
cocoa beans get squashed and mixed
with milk and sugar and that makes chocolate."

Lola says,
"Maybe I will grow one of
those cocoa bean trees
and make chocolate
myself."

So I say,
"I don't think it's so **easy**, Lola.
I saw this one really good
programme on the television
and it showed how
cocoa farmers
in Africa
work really,
really **hard**.

They have to look after the trees and pick the pods

and they take the cocoa beans out of the pods

and **dry** them in

And then, after maybe perhaps ten days, they put all the beans in sacks

and sell them to the chocolate factory."

the very hottish sun.

Charlie

Lola says,
"Ooh that sounds like an **absolutely**, really hard job."

And I say,
"It is. And sometimes the farmers don't even
get paid very much money for
picking all those millions
and catrillions of
cocoa beans."

Lola says,
"Oh that is
          NOT very fair."

And I say,
        "I know, but Mum says it is possible
to help the farmers get paid more.
          All you have to do is buy chocolate
with a special label on
          that says Fairtrade."

I say,
"You can actually even find the label on lots of
other things too and it means that the farmers
have always been paid a fair amount of money.
You can get orange juice
which is fairtrade...

and cereals
and bananas
and honey.

You can get
    Fairtrade nuts...

and fruit and cookies and
    chewy bars for your lunchbox.

There is tea and coffee and sugar
        and jam and sweets and flowers.

You can even buy fairtrade cotton t-shirts
            and footballs."

Use the special **fairtrade** sticker sheet at the back of the book and fill the **shelves** with lots of **fairtrade** things.

What should Charlie and Lola choose for their **dinner**?

What do you think **Sizzles** would like?

Charlie is looking for a **present** for **Marv**. Can you help him find something?

Can you see something sweet for **Lotta**?

Find a new **dress** for Lola.

When we get back from the shop
I say, "Lola, can I have a piece of chocolate?"
And she says, "I have gobbled it all up."
And I say,
"That's completely NOT fair."